Smith

Edda Reinl THE LITTLE SNAKE

Edda Reinl

The
Little
Snake

Neugebauer Press USA

A little green snake once lived near a meadow.
One morning as the sun sent its warming beams down upon the earth,
the little snake woke up.
She slipped from her bed of smooth stones and began to explore.

The meadow was deserted,
and the only creatures the snake could see
were the birds moving across the deep blue sky.
But the birds did not even notice the little green snake.

Suddenly the snake saw a grasshopper sitting on a leaf.
Before the curious snake could get a good look at her new friend,
the startled grasshopper jumped away.

Next the little snake came upon a family of mice.
They were eating some corn for breakfast,
but when they saw her they were afraid too,
and they scurried away.
So the snake slid off alone through the wide meadow,
and wandered back to her home among the smooth stones.

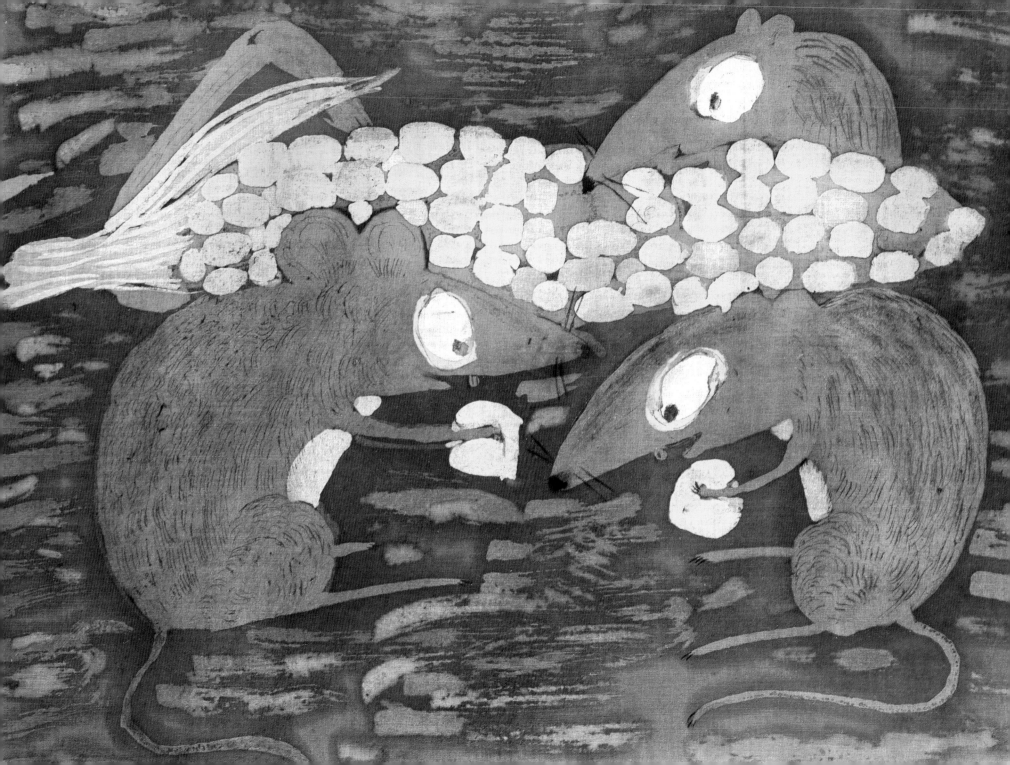

When the little snake was almost home,
she noticed something shining brightly through the waving grasses.
Carefully the snake moved closer.
A rare and lovely flower had blossomed in the bright sunshine.
The snake stood up to take a better look, and thought:
"How charming and beautiful this flower is!"
The beauty of the flower gave the little snake so much joy
that she decided to care for the flower and protect it forever.
Every day the snake lovingly watched over the flower,
and she even cleaned the summer dust off of its leaves.

Once a careless chicken was chasing a fly,
and it ran straight towards the flower.
Quickly the snake rose up and hissed loudly.
This frightened the chicken so much that it squawked
and fluttered away, leaving the beautiful flower safe and sound.

Another morning the snake found a dazzling butterfly
resting gently right on top of the blossom.
The flower and the butterfly swayed together in the breeze,
and the snake felt very sad.
It looked as though the flower had found a new friend.
The butterfly flew away after a few minutes,
but the little green snake thought:
"Has the flower forgotten about me?"

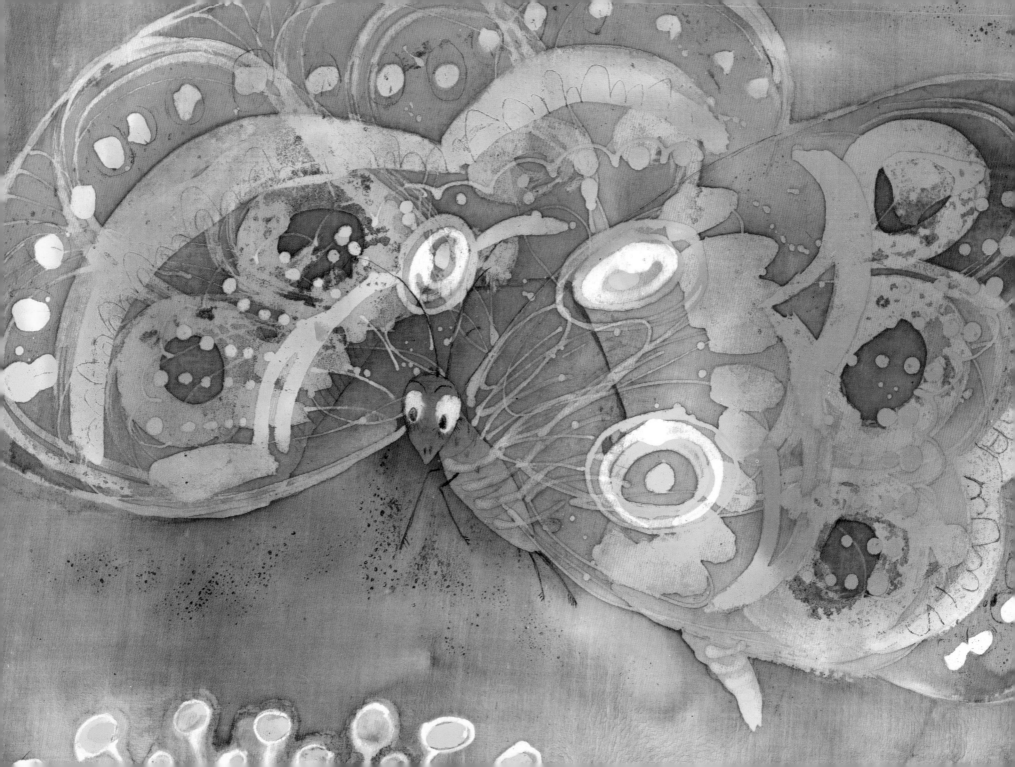

People walked through the meadow now and then.
Several times their big shoes almost trampled the flower,
but the little snake continued to guard it very carefully.

One evening it grew so cool
that the birds nestled together on their branches to stay warm.
The little snake thought her flower would be safe through the night,
so she slithered away into her warm hole among the smooth stones.

In the darkest, quietest part of the night,
a lost sheep wandered into the meadow.
It was eating blades of grass and leaves,
and with one quick bite the beautiful flower was gone.
When the little snake went to visit her flower in the morning,
all she found was the broken stalk.
This made the snake feel so sad
that the whole world seemed dull and empty.
As she crept back to her hole she thought:
"Even though it is gone,
I shall never forget the beauty of my flower and how I loved it."
But then something wonderful began to happen to the little green snake.

She thought so long and so lovingly about her beautiful flower
that her own appearance slowly changed.
If you visit the meadow today, the flowers and animals
will tell you about the little snake that they all love.
She is the lonely one who glides gently through the grass,
and she is as charming and as radiant as a flower.

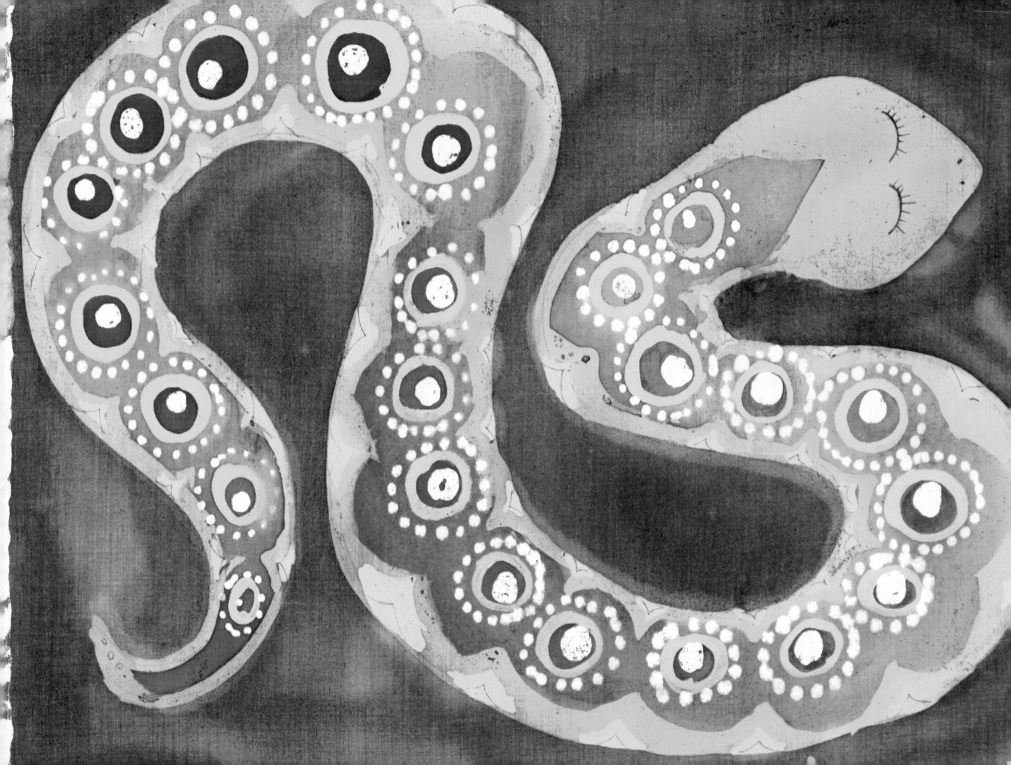